For François, for Marie

Dominique Blaizot

For Lionel

Stéphanie Blanchart

MYRIAD BOOKS LIMITED
35 Bishopsthorpe Road, London SE26 4PA

First published in 2000 by
MIJADE PUBLICATIONS
16-18, rue de l'Ouvrage
5000 Namur-Belgium

Translation: Lisa Pritchard

ISBN 1 84746 035 6

Printed in China

Little Scribbles

Dominique Blaizot

Stéphanie Blanchart

MYRIAD BOOKS LIMITED

Tonight, just as he always does, Dad asks
Frankie: "Shall I read you a story?"

And just as he always does,
Frankie says: "Oh no!"

It makes Dad sad that Frankie always says: "Oh no!"

Frankie never wants a story. He'd rather sing a song

… or have a tickle or a rough-and-tumble with Dad

or best of all, have a long, long cuddle with Mum until he goes to sleep.

"Why not?" asks Dad.

"I don't like stories because there are lots of scribbles in books."

"Whatever do you mean, scribbles?" asks Dad.
He picks up a book.

"Take a look. This one is brand new. There aren't any scribbles – just lovely pictures of a rabbit, an owl and a squirrel. Look."

"Yes there are," says Frankie. "Look, there are scribbles everywhere."

"Those aren't scribbles," says Dad. "Look, there are lines and curves. When you put them together they make letters. When you put the letters together they make words, and when you put all the words together they make a story."

"When you know how to read you can read everything: a bedtime story, the postcard from Grandma, even your letter from Santa Claus about the toys he's going to bring."

"Santa Claus learnt to read when he went to school. So now he can read the letters that children send him asking for special Christmas presents. Otherwise how would he know what the letters said?"

"I still think it looks like scribbles," Frankie says. "Make up a story in your head. Susie's dad doesn't read books, he just makes them up. I want a story like that."

So while Frankie snuggles down in bed, Dad makes up a story.

It's all about Martians who rescue a princess from the dragon, and the pirates who own the dragon and want to steal the princess's treasure…

It is a very complicated story, and Frankie falls asleep before Dad has finished it.

The next morning on the way to work, Dad thinks up another story. This one is much shorter and simpler.

So that evening, Dad tells Frankie the new story. It's all about Joe, a little bear who has lost his pot of honey.

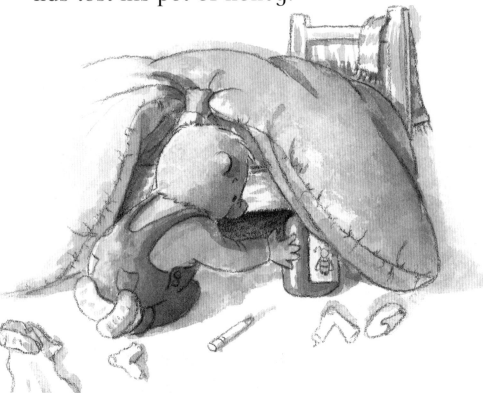

He wants to swap it for a skipping rope with his friend Laila.

Joe looks everywhere. At last he finds the pot of honey under his bed, and Laila swaps it for her skipping rope.

They are both happy: Laila eats the honey while Joe learns how to skip.

Laila tells Joe what to do.
She says he eats too much honey –
he might get a big fat bottom.
And it can be difficult to skip well
if you have a big fat bottom!

Joe keeps on practising.
He skips and skips, and
while he skips, Laila eats
honey. By the time Laila
has finished the pot, Joe
can skip!

The next evening, when Dad says, "Bedtime! What shall we do? Sing a song? Read a story?" Frankie asks for the story about the two little bears.

So Dad tells the story about Joe and the pot of honey he finds in his sock drawer and swaps for a skipping rope.

"No, Dad, you got it wrong!" says Frankie. "He didn't find it in his sock drawer, it was under his bed!"

The next evening, Frankie wants the same story. So Dad tells him about Joe, who swaps his skipping rope for some red and yellow lollipops.

"No, Dad, you got it wrong!" says Frankie. "He didn't swap it for lollipops, he swapped it for some honey. Bears don't know where to get lollipops, but they do know where to find honey!"

"Oh, of course!" says Dad. "I got it wrong. It's a good thing you were here. Shall I start again?"

The next evening Dad is late.
There's a problem at work so
he can't get home in time
to tell the story of the
two little bears.

Mum says, "Bedtime! Who would like a great big cuddle?"

Frankie replies, "Me! But first I want to hear the story of the two little bears."

"Which book is that in?" asks Mum.

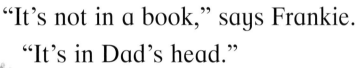

"It's not in a book," says Frankie.
"It's in Dad's head."

"Darling, if it is in Dad's head, I don't know it. He'll tell you his story tomorrow."

So Frankie has to settle for the story of Little Red Riding Hood and the big bad wolf. It's a bit scarier than Dad's story.

The next evening at bedtime, Dad says "Which story would you like this evening?"

Frankie answers, "The one about the two little bears, because Mum didn't know it yesterday."

"That's because I made it up and it's still in my head," says Dad.

"That's what Mum told me," Frankie says.

"Do you know how Mum could tell you the story that I made up?" asks Dad.

"Does she have to look under your hair?" asks Frankie, taking a good look at Dad's head.

" No," laughs Dad. "It's much simpler than that. I'll just write the story down on a piece of paper. Mum knows how to read, so she can read you the story as often as you want it."

"So Mum knows how to read those scribbles?"

"They aren't scribbles," says Dad. "The lines and curves will make letters, and the letters will make a story about our two little bears who skipped and ate honey."

"So Mum will be able to tell me your story?"

"Yes, she will. When you have a story in your head, write it down and Mum can read it as often as you like! And when I read it I won't get muddled up about who did what."

"But there are so many books," says Frankie. "Mum will have to learn all the other stories in all the other books. She will never be able to learn them all!"

"No, Frankie, when you learn to read you can read any book. You don't have to learn the story off by heart. Once you know how to read you can read any book you want, any time."

So Frankie asks Dad to show him.

Dad picks up a piece of paper and
a pencil. He writes down the story
about the two little bears
with the pot of honey
and the skipping rope.

Frankie watches Dad's scribbles. The lines and curves march tidily across the page. They don't really look like scribbles at all.

After a while, Dad says, "I've finished. Go and fetch Mum."

Frankie races into the kitchen and shouts, "Mum! Mum! Come and see!"

In Frankie's bedroom, Daddy is waiting with the sheet of paper he's written on. He gives it to Mum.

And Mum starts to read it…

And it works, it really works! When Mum finishes reading the story out loud, Frankie whispers, "It's all there, exactly the story that Daddy had in his head."

"Is that what you go to school for?"

"Yes, that's why you go to school. It's the best place to learn to read. And when you've learnt to read, you can have so much fun."

"You can read anything you want," says Frankie. "Bedtime stories, the postcard from Grandma, even Santa's letter about the toys he's going to bring."

"Yes," said Dad. "When you can read and write, you can talk to people everywhere, all over the world."

Frankie puts his head on the pillow. He asks Mum for a great big cuddle because today he discovered that reading is one of the best things that can happen to a child. It's one of life's big adventures.